INDIAN CHILDREN'S FAVOURITE STORIES

For Chand, Bela and Suraj—who fill my life and give me room to grow.

INDIAN CHILDREN'S FAVOURITE STORIES

retold by Rosemarie Somaiah
illustrated by Ranjan Somaiah

TUTTLE PUBLISHING
Tokyo • Rutland, Vermont • Singapore

India is a large, beautiful and very complex land with over a billion people. Its folklore, legends and mythology are a richly woven tapestry. Individual stories, like threads, weave in and out and shimmer or shine brilliantly, but it is often difficult to know where they begin and end. What is more, their colours seem to change with the light! As these stories evolved over hundreds of years over a very large geographical area, and have been told orally for generations, there are a myriad of versions—some strange, some funny—but all completely fascinating.

Some stories in this book are based on folklore and the common man. The motifs remain the same though the details may change. The wise man, the foolish man, the trickster and the clown—the popularity of these characters is undiminished.

Other stories have religious connotations. While these stories can hold their own on any bookshelf of myths and legends, it is important to remember that they form the core of a way of life that continues to this day.

All the major religions have followers in India. However, the majority of Indians are Hindus. To attempt to explain the rich philosophy of Hindusim is difficult. Still, one must begin somewhere.

Most Hindus believe in the concept of one Supreme Being, who in stories is given different names and attributes, resulting in the creation of characters called *devas.* In English, devas are loosely referred to as "gods" and "goddesses".

The three most popular male representations of the Supreme Being in Hindu mythology are Brahma, the Creator; Vishnu, the Preserver; and Shiva, the Destroyer. However, Shiva embodies many contrasts, for he can conquer death as well as destroy. Many of the heroes in myths and legends, such as Rama and Krishna, are human incarnations of Vishnu, the Preserver.

The female counterparts to these representatives are Saraswati, Goddess of Learning; Lakshmi, Goddess of Light; and Parvati, who, like Shiva, is full of contrasts. She may be seen either as a perfect wife or the fearsome goddess Kali.

The antagonists or villains in these stories are the demons called *rakshasas,* or *asuras,* who usually represent evil.

Both the devas and rakshasas, or asuras, can have magic powers, including the power to grant blessings or to curse. They can change their shapes and each of them usually has special skills.

On occasion, the devas, usually representatives of good, may make mistakes and the evil rakshasas or asuras can be heroic. When this happens, the deva may temporarily lose some power, and the rakshasa may gain some. In this way, the universe maintains a fragile balance.

Folktales, legends and mythology alike, these stories truly come to life again when they are retold or passed on from generation to generation as they have been for thousands of years.

Published by Tuttle Publishing,
an imprint of Periplus Editions (HK) Ltd,
with editorial offices at 364 Innovation Drive,
North Clarendon, VT 05759-9436, USA and
130 Joo Seng Road #06-01, Singapore 368357

LCC Card No: 2006931662
ISBN 13: 978-0-8048-3687-6
ISBN 10: 0-8048-3687-6

First printing, 2006
Printed in Malaysia

10 09 08 07 06
5 4 3 2 1

DISTRIBUTED BY:

North America, Latin America & Europe
Tuttle Publishing,
364 Innovation Drive,
North Clarendon, VT 05759-9436, USA
Tel: 1 (802) 773 8930 Fax: 1 (802) 773 6993
Email: info@tuttlepublishing.com
Website: www.tuttlepublishing.com

Asia Pacific
Berkeley Books Pte Ltd,
130 Joo Seng Road #06-01,
Singapore 368357
Tel: (65) 6280 1330 Fax: (65) 6280 6290
Email: inquiries@periplus.com.sg
Website: www.periplus.com

Japan
Tuttle Publishing,
Yaekari Building 3F, 5-4-12 Osaki,
Shinagawa-ku, Tokyo 141-0032
Tel: (03) 5437 0171 Fax: (03) 5437 0755
Email: tuttle-sales@gol.com

CONTENTS

Munna and the Grain of Rice

"Munna, where are you?"

"Here, Ma!" Munna replied. "I am playing with the elephants."

Munna, the elephant keeper's daughter, lived behind the palace grounds. She had never been to school and couldn't afford any toys. So instead, she played with what was around her—sand, sticks and stones—and made friends with birds and animals, and even insects.

She spent many happy hours with the elephants that her family cared for and loved deeply. Sometimes she rode on their backs, pretending that she was a Rani—a queen.

Munna liked to observe everything around her. She would examine the legs of insects and the wings of butterflies; peer closely at the leaves on the trees and the grains of rice on the stalks of paddy; press her ear against the broad sides of the elephants and listen to the rumblings in the stomachs of these gentle giants. She would even count the hairs on their tails!

But life in the small kingdom where Munna lived was not easy. The Raja—the king, would say, "I rule my kingdom fairly. I care for my people and I am wise and just. I am a good Raja!

The farmers in the kingdom were not so sure. They planted rice, working with bent backs in the fields all day.

One day the Raja ordered, "From now on, you will bring all your rice to me, except what you need to feed yourselves. I will keep it safe for you in my granary." The farmers had no choice. They did as they were told. And every year the Raja allowed them just enough rice to keep body and soul together.

But one year, the rain did not fall and there was a famine. The farmers had no food to give the Raja, or to feed themselves. They waited in vain for the Raja to give them some rice. "But I cannot give you the rice, or there will be none left for me," said the Raja. "A king cannot go hungry, or no one will call him Raja!" The people did not dare say anything.

Munna, with her bright eyes and enquiring mind, watched as the hungry people starved and grew sad. She wondered what she could do.

One day, a servant loaded sacks of rice from the granary onto the back of an elephant. He led the elephant towards the royal kitchen. But there was a tiny hole in one of the sacks and some grains of rice fell through. Munna picked them up. She gathered them carefully in her skirt and took them back to the Raja.

The Raja decided to reward her for her honesty. He offered her gold, silver and jewels. But Munna bowed low and said humbly, "Your Majesty, I am small and I need very little. All I want is one grain of rice."

The Raja was surprised. "Nonsense! You must have more. After all, I am the Raja."

"Your Majesty, if it be your royal command," said the girl, "I will accept more, but only for one month. Give me one grain of rice on the first day, and on every day following give me only twice what you have given me the day before."

The Raja thought it was really too little. But she was, after all, a simple, foolish girl—an elephant keeper's daughter!—and so he agreed.

So, on the first day, Munna accepted one grain of rice. On the second day she accepted two grains of rice, on the third day, four, on the fourth day, eight, and so on. She saved them all.

On the tenth day, Munna was given five hundred and twelve grains—about one handful of rice. Together with all that she had received so far, she now had one thousand and twenty-three grains. She gave it all to her mother, who put it aside carefully.

On the fourteenth day, which was halfway through the traditional Indian lunar month, Munna was presented with eight thousand, one hundred and ninety-two grains of rice.

By the next day, there was enough rice to fill four bowls—four bowls for three people! Her mother cooked just as much as the three of them, with their small stomachs, could eat. That night they shared a meal of rice. It was delicious!

On the twentieth day, Munna was given sixteen small bags of rice. Together with what had come earlier, she now had almost thirty-two small bags of rice. On the twenty-first day, she received more than a million grains of rice—one million, forty-eight thousand, five hundred and seventy-six grains, in fact. Enough to fill a large basket. It looked so big in their tiny little hut! The family moved around it carefully.

On the twenty-fifth day, she received sixteen baskets. Had they been placed one on top of the other, the pile would have been as high as an elephant. It was a good thing it did not rain then, for the soldiers arranged the baskets neatly beside the elephants in the yard in front of the hut. As they did, they wondered at the cleverness of the little girl.

On the last day of the month, the twenty-eighth day, Munna received one hundred and twenty-eight baskets of rice. The Raja was astounded, for that was the entire contents of his granary! He looked around. There was not a single grain of rice left for him.

But Munna was smart. She knew how difficult it would for the people to live under an unhappy ruler.

"I do not need all this rice, Your Majesty," said Munna. "I cannot eat it all, and I have no place to keep it. May I request that you, as a good and kind king, use it to feed the hungry people of your kingdom?"

The Raja promised to do so. As the people of the kingdom received enough rice to fill their bellies, they bowed to the Raja. But in their hearts, they thanked their own little Munna—the girl with a clever head and a truly generous heart.

The Birth of Krishna

Long, long ago, it is said, gods and goddesses, demons and humans all lived together on this earth. Though they had their own worlds, the gods—or devas, and the demons—or asuras, would sometimes take the form of human beings. They would be born to human mothers and fathers and seem like ordinary human children. But the asuras would reveal their true natures with their evil deeds. And the devas would reveal their true natures when the time came for them to solve great problems, or to right grievous wrongs.

In such a time, there lived a cruel prince called Kamsa, who some people say was an asura. Kamsa had no sisters and brothers, but he had a cousin called Devaki, a beautiful girl whom he loved as dearly as a sister.

Now, Kamsa was a strange man. As long as he was in the company of good men, he would behave like a good man. But at other times, he would forget himself and his evil nature would take possession of him.

Unfortunately, many of his ministers were asuras, demons in the shape of men, and they constantly goaded him to behave in evil ways.

The day came when his cousin, Devaki, grew into a young maiden ready to be married. A gentle and kind nobleman called Vasudeva seemed the perfect match.

Their wedding was celebrated with great joy. The festivities were grand, and when the time came for the bride to be taken to her new home, it is said that a hundred golden chariots, four hundred elephants and an enormous army stood by to escort the newlyweds.

As he watched the couple get ready to depart, Kamsa felt sad to see Devaki leave. He went to their chariot and asked the charioteer to get down. He had decided, as a gesture of his affection for Devaki, to drive the chariot himself. He picked up the reins and they set off.

They were riding along when suddenly there was a burst of thunder. Then a great voice boomed from the heavens: "Kamsa, your death has been decided. The eighth child born to Devaki will be the one who will slay you!"

Kamsa was seized with great fear. In an instant, he had drawn out his sword and grabbed the frightened Devaki by her hair. "Ha!" he roared. "Only if she lives to see that day! I shall slay her before that!" He held the sword at Devaki's neck.

Vasudeva, horrified, grabbed Kamsa's hand and pleaded, "Kamsa, don't! You love Devaki as a younger sister. She has done you no harm. You should be the one to protect her!"

But Kamsa pulled away. Seeing that his pleas fell on deaf ears, Vasudeva made one last desperate attempt to save his bride.

"Kamsa, I promise you, you will have nothing to fear from Devaki," he said. "I hereby swear that I will hand over every one of our children to you as soon as they are born."

Knowing that this was the promise of a nobleman, Kamsa considered it for a while. Then, realizing that the crime he was about to commit in front of so many people would show him to be a demon, he agreed to let Devaki go.

Soon enough, a child was born to Vasudeva and Devaki. As promised, Vasudeva took the child to Kamsa. At first Kamsa thought he had nothing to fear. After all, he had been warned only of the eighth child. However, confused by all the different advice he was given by his asura ministers, he soon killed the child.

Having done that, it seemed as if evil finally took control of him. Kamsa even imprisoned his father, King Ugrasena, and took over his kingdom. He caught Vasudeva and Devaki as well. They, too, were thrown into prison.

Then began a time of great sorrow and horror in the kingdom. Over the terrible years, Devaki bore six children, and each of them was killed. By then, even the gods could not bear to stand by and watch. When the seventh child began to grow in her belly, they decided to act.

The gods moved Devaki's child into the womb of Vasudeva's other wife Rohini, who lived in the village of Gokul. Kamsa was told that Devaki's seventh child was stillborn, or dead at birth.

More time passed, and it was finally time for Devaki's eighth child to be born. Kamsa grew impatient and restless. He ordered that Vasudeva and Devaki be bound and chained to the walls of their cell. Everyone waited.

Many different things are said about the night this special baby was born. Some say that it was a beautiful night like none other—peaceful and calm with clear skies and stars glowing bright. It is said that lotuses were in full bloom in the lakes and the fragrant flowers in the gardens waved gently in the breeze. Birds began to sing, they say, and peacocks began to dance in the forests. Some say the gods even showered flowers from the sky to express their joy.

Others say that there was a great storm on this night, with thunder and lightning, as if the world knew that something of great importance was about to happen. It was a strange and magical night, a night when all things were possible.

At midnight, Devaki's eighth child, a boy who would be called Krishna, entered the world. When Devaki first laid her eyes on the baby, she knew that this was indeed a special child. Vasudeva knew this too, and realized that they would have to save Krishna somehow. But, how? They were prisoners. Vasudeva tugged desperately at the chains that bound him. How he longed to hold his newborn child in his arms!

Just then, much to Vasudeva's surprise, the chains fell off his hands and legs. Trembling, he picked up his child, kissed him and nestled him against his shoulder. Turning, the wondering Vasudeva saw the great doors of his prison open silently and, as he stepped out carefully, he found that all the guards had fallen into a deep sleep. Quickly, Vasudeva slipped through the quiet corridors. The child Krishna seemed to know how dangerous this moment was, for he did not so much as whimper.

"I shall take him to my friend Nanda, in Gokul," Vasudeva thought. He hurried to the river, but it was in full spate. The flood-waters thrashed the banks. But as Vasudeva stood at the river's edge, the waters parted in front of him and a path right through the riverbed led him to the other bank.

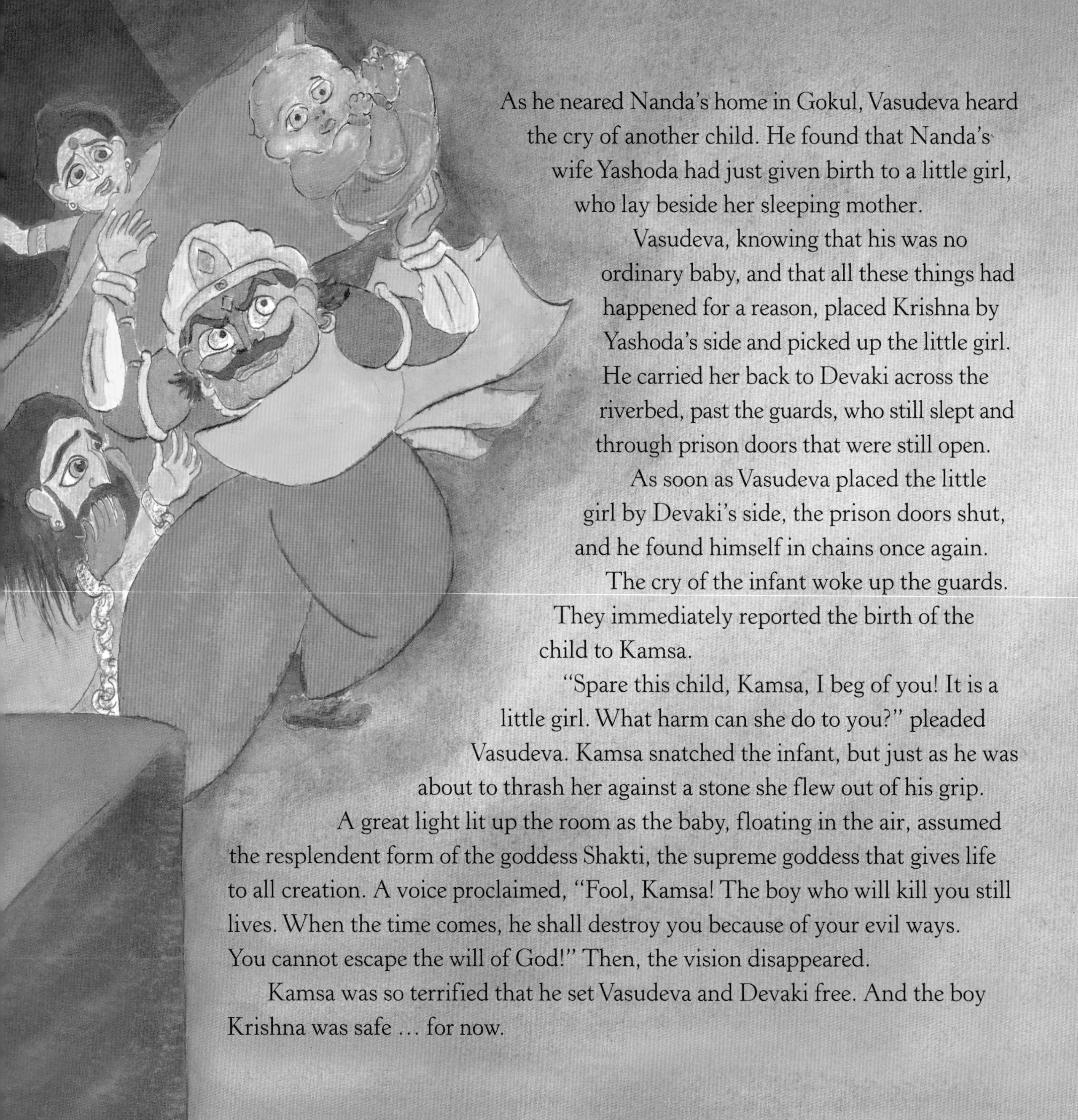

As he neared Nanda's home in Gokul, Vasudeva heard the cry of another child. He found that Nanda's wife Yashoda had just given birth to a little girl, who lay beside her sleeping mother.

Vasudeva, knowing that his was no ordinary baby, and that all these things had happened for a reason, placed Krishna by Yashoda's side and picked up the little girl. He carried her back to Devaki across the riverbed, past the guards, who still slept and through prison doors that were still open.

As soon as Vasudeva placed the little girl by Devaki's side, the prison doors shut, and he found himself in chains once again.

The cry of the infant woke up the guards. They immediately reported the birth of the child to Kamsa.

"Spare this child, Kamsa, I beg of you! It is a little girl. What harm can she do to you?" pleaded Vasudeva. Kamsa snatched the infant, but just as he was about to thrash her against a stone she flew out of his grip.

A great light lit up the room as the baby, floating in the air, assumed the resplendent form of the goddess Shakti, the supreme goddess that gives life to all creation. A voice proclaimed, "Fool, Kamsa! The boy who will kill you still lives. When the time comes, he shall destroy you because of your evil ways. You cannot escape the will of God!" Then, the vision disappeared.

Kamsa was so terrified that he set Vasudeva and Devaki free. And the boy Krishna was safe … for now.

No Ordinary Lad

The evil king Kamsa was greatly upset. He had been told that the boy who would grow up to kill him still lived. But he did not know where the child was.

He consulted his ministers, who, being asuras, or demons in disguise, advised him to kill all the newborn babies in and around the kingdom. Kamsa called upon Poothana, a horribly big, ugly, evil asura, and asked her to carry out the task.

Meanwhile, in the village of Gokul, where the baby Krishna now lived, the word had gone around.

"Nanda and Yashoda have a beautiful baby boy!"
"Yes, and he has a lovely name too—Krishna!"

All the villagers came to visit, and the happy parents distributed sweets and presents to them. Somehow, the birth seemed to bring great joy to the village. People sang and danced to celebrate the happy event.

But the asura Poothana, disguising herself by taking on the form of a lovely woman, wandered around looking for the baby. When she finally found the house where Nanda and Yashoda rejoiced in their new son, Poothana slipped inside. In a soft, charming voice, she asked for permission to hold the child, as many visitors did.

Yashoda, surrounded by love and kindness, did not suspect a thing. She left Krishna and Poothana alone for a few minutes. Poothana picked up baby Krishna and put him to her breast, which was full of deadly poison. But the baby Krishna sucked out all the poison without coming to any harm. Not only that, he also sucked all the life right out of the horrible, evil woman!

When Yashoda came back a few minutes later, she found Krishna gurgling contentedly beside the lifeless Poothana, who had regained her true demon form.

People wondered at the power of this special baby.

Soon Kamsa heard of the death of Poothana. But he was not about to give up yet. He sent another asura, Trinavarta who had the power to control storms and whirlwinds, to kill the baby.

Krishna, the holy child, had a sense of the approaching danger. He sat on his mother's lap, but Yashoda found him suddenly becoming heavier and heavier. Finally, she could take his weight no longer. "Am I so tired?" she wondered. Gasping with the effort, Yashoda put Krishna down on the ground and went to call for help.

Trinavarta, who had just arrived, turned into a whirlwind and began to raise a terrible dust storm. Huge swirls of dust and sand rose and filled the air. It got into everyone's eyes and blocked their noses. They struggled to cover their faces. Such a storm had never been seen before!

Trinavarta lifted Krishna and began to fly higher and higher in the twisting, whirling sandstorm. But he found it difficult to carry the little boy, who was growing heavier and heavier. Krishna stretched out his chubby hand and clutched the throat of the demon, choking him. The asura fell to the ground like a big stone, crashing down onto a rock—dead.

The anxious villagers later found Krishna lying beside the lifeless body of the demon.

Krishna grew up to be an adorable little fellow, with shiny dark skin, chubby cheeks and bright, beautiful eyes. Like any doting mother, Yashoda dressed him carefully and he always wore a beautiful peacock feather in his headdress. His favourite companion was his older brother, Balarama, the seventh son who had been whisked away to Gokul before he had even been born. The two boys were inseparable.

But, oh, Krishna was naughty! He would play every prank he could, but was so sweet afterwards that he could usually charm his way out of trouble. Still, there was many a time when he tried even the patience of his adoring mother.

Yashoda and her friends were milkmaids who reared cows. All the milkmaids worked hard every day, churning the extra milk into butter and making ghee.

Now, Krishna loved milk, curds, butter and ghee, and no matter how much his mother willingly gave him, he was always trying to get a little more.

Krishna found ways to sneak into his house, after his mother had chased him away from the pot of butter and sent him out to play with Balarama and his other friends. Not only that, he was more than happy to treat everyone else's home as his own. No matter what anyone tried, they could not hide butter or milk from Krishna. Soon, he was even drinking milk directly from the cow!

"But mother, the cow willingly gave it to me," said Krishna.

It was true, after all. The cow had stood still, seemingly letting the boy drink his fill.

Still, his poor mother soon got used to listening to a long list of complaints from all the neighbours. She chided Krishna, warned him, scolded him and punished him, but no matter what she said or did, Krishna had an answer to everything.

Krishna was Krishna!

One day just before a festival, Krishna kept getting in his mother's way. He meddled in her preparations and upset her pots of curds, making her so cross that she decided to punish him. She tied him up with rope to a large mortar, his hands behind his back. This mortar, a heavy piece of stone that was almost as tall as Krishna, stood outside the house and was to be used for pounding grain into flour.

Krishna waited and waited. Soon he began to get bored, so he tried to think of a way to get loose.

"I know! I will go to Balarama. He will surely untie me!"

No sooner had he thought of it, Krishna began to move. Dragging the enormous weight of the mortar behind him easily, he made his way down to the fields to find Balarama.

Unfortunately, he had to go through some trees and soon found himself trapped. The mortar had wedged itself between the broad trunks of two tall trees.

He paused for a minute and then tugged impatiently at the weight, hoping that he could dislodge the mortar. With an enormous CRASH! the trees came tumbling down, and Krishna went on his way.

As the news of this event spread, a crowd gathered to marvel at the great strength of this young boy.

"This Krishna is no ordinary lad!" they agreed.

But it would take many years, many stories, and many magical feats before people realized that Krishna was in fact a deva in human form.

The Story of Rama

The gods, or devas, were upset. Milling around, talking all at once, they complained to Brahma, the Creator.

"Ravana, the ten-headed rakshasa, has grown too proud. He is an insufferable bully! He and his gang of demon hooligans strut around scoffing at everything sacred. They pillage and plunder and ill-treat even the priests and the women."

"You, Brahma, are the one who granted him the boon that makes him so strong. It is you that we now turn to for help!"

Brahma considered the matter. Yes, it was he who had granted Ravana's prayer, although he hadn't really had a choice in the matter. Ravana had managed, with extreme penance and the practice of yoga, to gain the power to slow the movement of the planets almost to a standstill. To save the universe, Brahma had had to allow him his wish. And so, as Ravana had requested, no deva, asura, gandhara, rakshasa, or other such being could destroy him. He had become invulnerable, invincible. Or, so he thought.

But Brahma told the devas that Ravana, in his arrogance, had not chosen his wish carefully. He had forgotten about the humans and the animals on earth. Perhaps Ravana had thought them too puny to fear.

The devas turned immediately to Lord Vishnu, the Preserver, and begged him to be born as a man—the man who would destroy Ravana.

Meanwhile on earth, the good king Dasaratha was preparing for a horse sacrifice. Dasaratha had many blessings—Ayodhya, the capital city of his kingdom, was magnificent. His people were happy, contented and virtuous and they loved him well. But the aging king was not happy. He had no children, no heir, no one to whom he could hand down his kingdom. And so he prepared the sacrifice and prayed for a son.

As ghee was poured into the fire and the flames shot up to meet it, there was a blinding flash. A figure, brilliant as the noonday sun, appeared with a golden bowl in his hands. He offered it to King Dasaratha and said, "Let your wives share the sweet delicacy in this bowl and they will be blessed with sons."

In time, four sons were born to Dasaratha's three wives, Kausalya, Kaikeyi and Sumithra.

Kausalya's son was called Rama and Kaikeyi's son was called Bharata. Sumithra, Dasaratha's youngest wife, gave birth to twins, whom they called Lakshmana and Shatruguna.

The young princes grew up to be strong, handsome young men who were brave and skilled in all the princely arts. But of them all, the most beloved was Rama.

One day, a wise and respected sage came to see Dasaratha. He had come for help. Ferocious rakshasas roamed around the forests in which he and the other holy men lived and prayed. They polluted the religious sacrifices and preyed on the people.

The sage wanted Rama to go with him to fight the rakshasas and protect the innocent.

The king was fearful. His favourite son was but sixteen years old and he knew not what the gods had planned for him. But, in the end, with the sage's assurance that no serious harm would befall Rama, the king agreed to let him go with the holy man. Lakshmana, Rama's favourite brother, was to go with them.

On the journey to the forest where he lived, the sage, who was a master of every weapon, trained the boys well in the art of war. In addition, he gave them special powers of their own. Soon, they had vanquished the rakshasas.

On the way home, the princes visited Janaka, the king of of the neighbouring kingdom, at his capital city of Mithila.

Janaka had a daughter, Sita. Believed to be the goddess Earth's gift to the noble king, Sita was divinely beautiful. And she was as good and virtuous as she was lovely.

Many princes had wished to marry her, but her father had set a test. He had a special bow, given to him by a god. It was so large and heavy that it could only be moved in a chariot with eight enormous wheels. Nobody had ever been able to lift the bow to string it, though many had tried. Janaka had declared that anyone who could accomplish this great feat could marry Sita.

To the amazement of all gathered, Rama lifted the bow with no effort at all. He strung it and drew back the string with ease, but it broke with a thunderclap so loud that it shook the earth.

The kingdom celebrated the marriage of Rama and Sita with great joy, and the heavens sent down showers of flowers to bless the wedding.

However, the lives of the royal couple would soon take the path the gods had determined for them.

King Dasaratha was now ready to hand down his kingdom to his eldest son, Rama, the rightful heir. All the people rejoiced at this welcome news and prepared for the coronation. That is, all the people except Kaikeyi, Dasaratha's second wife, who was greatly displeased. She said to the king, "Once, when you were wounded in battle and at death's door, I cured you. You then promised me two boons that I could use at my pleasure. If you are truly a king, grant me my wishes now or all men will forever despise you!"

And so, she forced Dasaratha to crown her son, Bharata, king instead of Rama.

She also made the heartbroken and desperate king order Rama, the son he adored, into exile. Rama was to live in the forest for fourteen years.

The people were greatly upset. Bharata even refused to accept the crown. Eveyone in the kingdom grieved, except Kaikeyi and Rama himself. The king had given his word, and Rama was determined to uphold the honour of his father's promise.

Rama gave up his life of luxury willingly. With simple clothes made of bark and little else, he set off for the forest. His devoted wife Sita and one of his brothers, Lakshmana, left as well, refusing to be parted from him.

Life was hard, but for many years Rama, Sita and Lakshmana were happy in the forest. They lived in a small hut and found joy in simple pleasures—the flowers, the trees and the songs of the birds.

But, trouble was in store.

One day, the terrifying Ravana heard about Rama—and the beautiful Sita. He decided to kidnap Sita and keep her for himself.

Ravana's powers allowed him to change his shape at will. He arranged for his friend to take the form of a shining golden deer with silver spots and horns that shone like jewels. This beautiful, gentle animal was to graze in the forest and lure Rama and Lakshmana away from Sita, whom they protected at all times.

Sita caught glimpses of the deer through the trees and was enchanted. "Rama, please capture it for me!" she begged. "Our time in the forest is almost done. When we return to the palace it will remind us of the wonderful years we have had here."

Leaving his brother to guard Sita, Rama went after the deer.

But as he neared it, he realized that he had been tricked, for the magic deer called out in a voice like Rama's, "Ah! Sita! Lakshmana! Save me!"

Sita, hearing the voice, was confused into thinking that Rama was in trouble. Despite Lakshmana's protests that it could be a trick, and that he had promised Rama to stay beside her, she insisted that he go to her husband, who needed help.

Meanwhile, the evil Ravana, pretending to be a holy man, came to the door of the hut where the three lived to ask for food. As was the custom, the good Sita invited him in. And so, alas, the ten-headed demon grabbed Sita, threw her in his flying chariot and carried her away to his mountaintop palace, which laid in Lanka, hundreds of miles away and across the sea.

While struggling with the demon as they travelled across the skies in his chariot, Sita managed to throw down the wildflowers from her hair and pieces of her jewellery. Tearfully, she prayed, "Rama, Lakshmana, please come to my rescue!"

When Rama and Lakshmana found Sita gone, Rama was heartbroken. They looked for her everywhere.

While searching, they reached the Land of the Monkey King, deep in the mountains. There they met his chief minister, Hanuman, son of the Wind God Vayu. Hanuman showed them the flowers and jewels that had been found scattered.

"These are the very flowers I gave her! These are her jewels!" said Rama excitedly.

Hanuman quickly became a firm friend. He did not know then, but this too had been decided by the gods. He and his companions, the monkeys and the bears, joined forces with Rama, and the search for Sita continued.

Different search parties travelled east and west, north and south.

Finally, Hanuman and his team came to where the land reached the sea and could go no further.

At the water's edge, they found flowers and jewels that could only have belonged to Sita. Hanuman realized that Ravana must have carried Sita across the waters. As they stared into the distance across the glistening waves, the richly jewelled city of Lanka shimmered into view. But how were they to cross to the other side of the sea?

It was then that Hanuman, grappling with the problem, began to realize his true powers. He stood on a mountain in deep concentration, and with every breath he took, he grew larger and larger. Finally, he took a gigantic leap.

All kinds of strange monsters reared up from the sea, blocking, biting, grabbing, grasping—all determined to stop him. But he evaded them and blazed across the sky like a comet.

Once Hanuman landed in Lanka, however, he used his new-found powers to shrink to a size no bigger than a cat, and made his way in secret to Sita. He wanted to be sure that she was safe.

He scampered in and around the magnificent city, through its streets and mansions, palaces and courtyards, searching for any sign of Sita. He had roamed through almost all of Lanka and was about to give up hope when he finally found her, trapped in a little garden surrounded by high walls and heavily guarded by Ravana's soldiers.

When Hanuman first spoke to her, Sita, who had never seen him before, was worried. What if it was but another trick? But Hanuman finally convinced her that he was Rama's friend.

Sita took out a jewel from a knot in her sari and gave it to Hanuman, saying, "Give this to my husband as a sign from me."

Hanuman travelled all the way back to the other side of the sea and handed the jewel to Rama. Rama's heart rejoiced to know that Sita was still alive.

Quickly, Rama, Lakshmana, Hanuman, and all their friends gathered their weapons and prepared to rescue Sita. Calling on the sea god to help calm the waters, they built a strong bridge over the sea so that the army could march across and enter Lanka.

Then, with the enemies on either side seemingly evenly matched, the war began.

And, oh, what a fearsome war it was! People say that such a war had never been seen before and will never be seen again.

Both Rama and Ravana possessed extraordinary skills and spectacular powers. And the relatives and allies in their armies were no ordinary mortals, either.

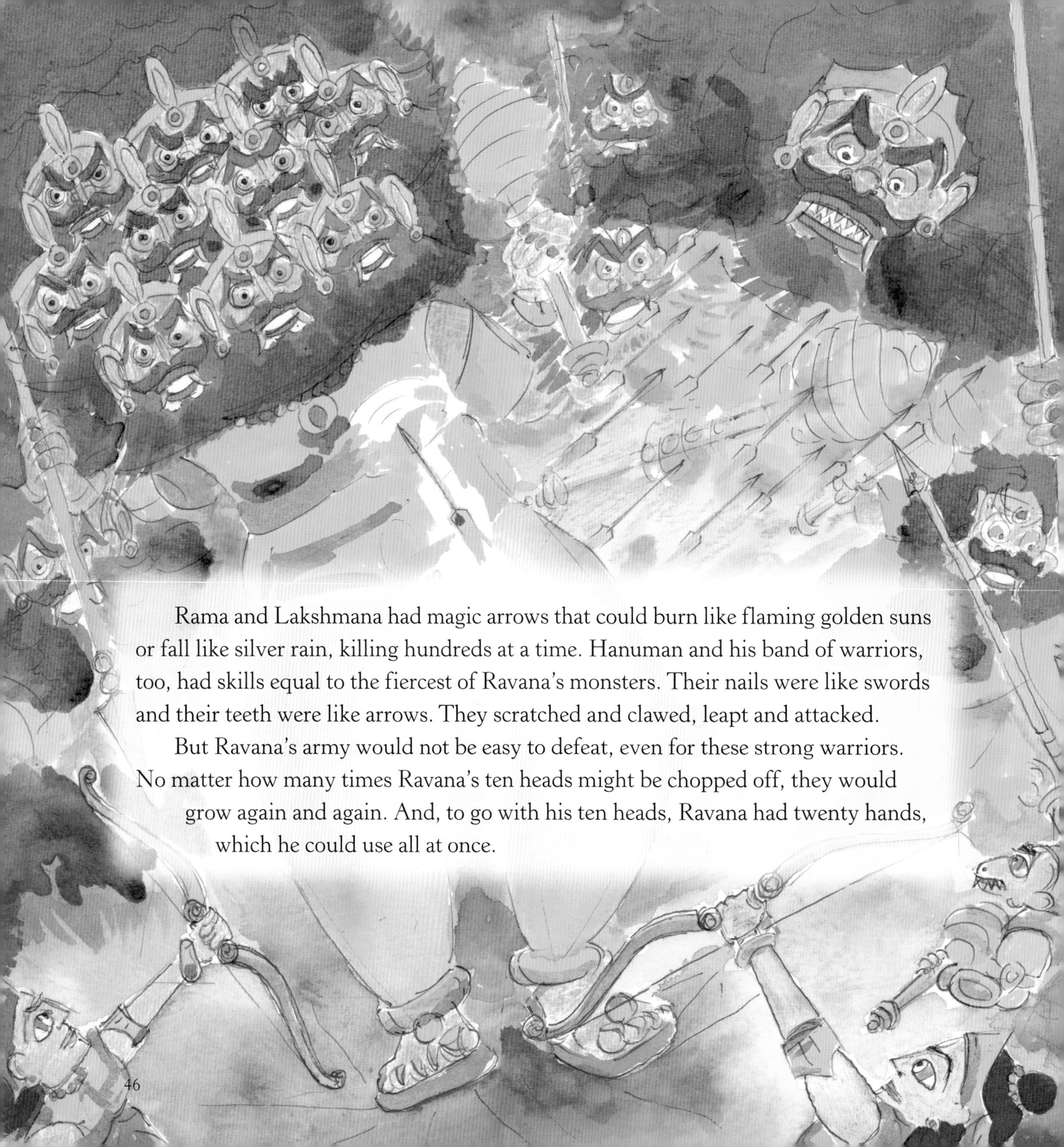

Rama and Lakshmana had magic arrows that could burn like flaming golden suns or fall like silver rain, killing hundreds at a time. Hanuman and his band of warriors, too, had skills equal to the fiercest of Ravana's monsters. Their nails were like swords and their teeth were like arrows. They scratched and clawed, leapt and attacked.

But Ravana's army would not be easy to defeat, even for these strong warriors. No matter how many times Ravana's ten heads might be chopped off, they would grow again and again. And, to go with his ten heads, Ravana had twenty hands, which he could use all at once.

Ravana's son, Indrajit was a master of magic. With spells and potions, he could conjure up shapes to confuse and befuddle his opponents. Another powerful fighter was Ravana's brother, Kumbakarna, who was the biggest giant the world had ever known. He could sleep for six months at a time, but when he awoke he would be so ravenous that he could devour entire armies at a time.

When these famous warriors met, the land, sea, sky and universe itself seemed to explode as incredible weapons flew in every direction.

Finally, Rama and Ravana faced each other. Rama drew his bow, and with unerring aim, he shot one splendid, flaming arrow straight into Ravana's heart, killing him.

With that, the war ended. Rama had finally accomplished what he had been born on earth to do.

The gods celebrated, trumpets blew, the air was scented with flowers that fell from the heavens.

Rama, Sita and Lakshmana, having been away for fourteen years, returned to the land of their birth to claim what was rightfully theirs.

Bharata, Rama's brother, welcomed him warmly. "Never have I sat on the throne, Rama. I have guarded it for you. You are the rightful king."

Rama took the throne, and was a good and wise ruler.

And that is the story of Rama, which will be told as long as the mountains shall stand and the rivers shall flow.

Sukhu and Dukhu

Long ago and far away, there lived a man who had two wives and two daughters. The elder wife's daughter was called Dukhu. Though she and her mother were good, kind and very hardworking, the man cared more for his younger wife and her lazy, spiteful daughter, Sukhu.

Sukhu and her mother knew this, so they treated Dukhu and her mother with scorn and made them do all the work, while they themselves did nothing but primp and preen, and try to look pretty.

One day the man died, and the younger wife drove Dukhu and her mother out of the house, saying, "You are the cause of all our sorrow!"

A kindly neighbour who took pity on them gave them shelter and an old spinning wheel. Every day, Dukhu and her mother struggled to spin, cook, clean, and do the chores around the little hut.

But one day, as Dukhu sat at the spinning wheel by the front door, dark clouds began to gather. A sudden gust of wind blew and—Poof!—carried away the wad of cotton she was about to spin into thread.

It was more than poor Dukhu could bear. She chased after that fluff of cotton, tears streaming down her face, as the wind called out, 'Dukhu…Dukhu…!'

The wind led her past a dirty cowshed. "MoooOO!" said the cow mournfully. "Help me, Dukhu!"

Dukhu looked at the cow, ankle-deep in dung. "Poor cow! You must be so uncomfortable." She brushed away her tears and stopped to clean and wash the shed. When she was done, she stroked the grateful cow and hurried on.

Outside the shed, the wind rose again, beckoning, leading her further away from home.

She came across a banana plant. Trailing vines and creepers wound around it so tightly that it could hardly stand. Its broad, flat leaves hung limply, and it called out, "Please help me, Dukhu!"

Dukhu looked at the plant. "You poor thing!" she said as she deftly removed the creepers. She scooped some water from a nearby stream in her palms and watered the plant as best she could. Then she hurried on.

The wind whipped round a little hill and as she followed it, further up the stream. Dukhu found an old horse, gaunt and bony, sighing deeply. Its saddle and bridle had been pulled so tight that it could not bend down to drink the water. "Please help me, Dukhu," it begged. "I am so thirsty."

"Oh, poor horse!" said Dukhu as she loosened the leather straps and buckles.

"That should make you feel better." And she hurried on.

The wind led her to the very edge of the village. Out there in the gathering gloom, it lifted her hair, tickled her cheeks and whispered softly in her ear, "Stand very still and look carefully, Dukhu. You will see what you should see." Then suddenly all was silent.

Dukhu squinted and stared out into the dusk till her eyes began to water. Slowly, the misty outlines of a distant palace swam into view through her tears. It shimmered and shone. It seemed so far and yet so near. Could she be imagining it?

She walked towards it timidly, worrying that it would disappear. Finally, she stood in an open doorway. She thought she heard a gentle voice call out, "Come in," but when Dukhu entered, there was nobody there.

She wandered through empty hallways and around large rooms with walls glowing palely white. Finally, she came to a small room at the far end of the palace.

Peering into it, she saw a hunched figure bent over a spinning wheel. An old woman sat there, her silver hair gleaming in the moonlight that streamed in through the window.

"So, you are finally here," said the old woman, turning to greet Dukhu.

Dukhu stepped forward. Respectfully, she reached out and touched the old lady's feet. Then she brought her palms back to touch her own head in a sign of reverence. She tried to speak, but no words came from her mouth. She knelt there, her head bowed.

The old lady reached out and stroked her hair gently. Then she helped Dukhu to her feet. "Never mind. I am the Mother of the Moon. Do not be afraid. Come with me." She led Dukhu to a pond in the garden. "Dip yourself in it twice, and you will get what you truly deserve."

Dukhu dipped herself in the water once. When she came out, she found she was no longer a plain village girl. She could barely recognize the beautiful face that was reflected in the water.

She dipped herself in the pond a second time.

Now she found that she was draped in the finest, softest muslin silk sari, its beautiful colours and patterns swirling gracefully around her. Gold necklaces circled her neck. Rubies and emeralds gleamed and glittered from the bracelets on her arms and the rings on her fingers. Pearls hung from her ears and a diamond flashed from her nose ring.

Then the Mother of the Moon led her back to the room and said, "Now eat, my child." And there, laid before her were delicious mounds of steaming rice dotted with raisins and nuts; curries rich with fragrant spices; light, hot bread, some crisp and some soft with melted butter and ghee; and sweets and desserts. It was much more than she could ever eat.

When she had had her fill, Dukhu bowed to give thanks. Then the Mother of the Moon showed her three treasure chests and said, "Choose one."

Dukhu, more than grateful for what she had so far received, chose the smallest one. Then, bidding the old lady goodbye, she left the palace.

As she passed the horse, it gave her a beautiful, sprightly young colt to take home with her. The banana plant gave her a bunch of golden bananas and a pot of gold coins. The cow gave her a healthy brown calf, which would provide Sukhu and her mother with fresh milk for the rest of their lives.

Dukhu thanked them all and made her way home.

Her poor mother was delighted to see her. Dukhu showed her all the presents the Mother of the Moon had given her. "And, oh! There's one more!" said Dukhu, as she remembered the small treasure chest.

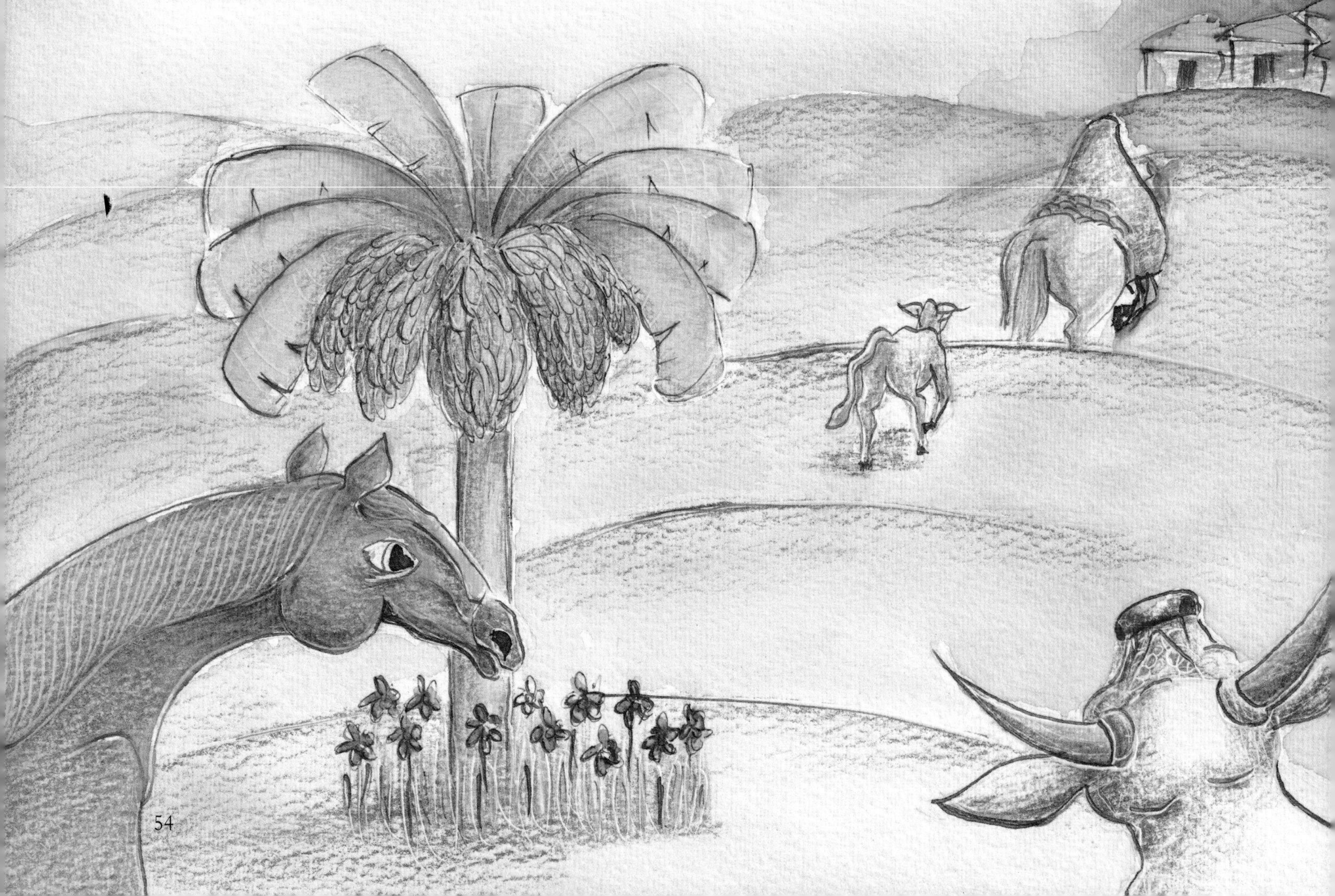

When she opened the chest, a handsome young man appeared in a puff of smoke. "I have come to marry you," he said, simply.

All Dukhu's friends and relatives were invited to her grand wedding. Even Sukhu and her mother came, curious to find out how Dukhu had become so wealthy.

Once they heard about the Mother of the Moon, Sukhu's mother wasted no time. She bought her daughter a spinning wheel, sat her outside their door and instructed her to cry loudly when the wind carried away her wad of cotton.

Just as her sister had done earlier, Sukhu followed the wind when it whisked away her cotton. But when the cow called out for help, she scorned it.

Tossing her head, she said haughtily, "Who do you think I am—a cowherd's daughter?" And she stomped on.

When she met the weak and withering banana tree, she said, "I'm no farmer's daughter. My hands are too soft for such tasks!" And she stamped her feet and flounced on.

When she met the horse, she shouted angrily, "Get out of my way, you old nag! Do you think I am a stable-hand? I am on my way to see the Mother of the Moon herself!" And she kicked the horse and strode on.

By the time she finally found the palace of the Mother of the Moon, she was tired, hungry and crosser than ever.

With one hand on her hips, she waved the other angrily at the silver-haired, hunched old woman and scolded, "The stupid wind has carried away my wad of cotton! And you'd better do something about it…or else!"

The old woman replied patiently, "Go to the pond that glistens with the reflection of the moon and dip yourself in it twice. Then you will get what you deserve. Remember, only twice, not more."

Sukhu hurried to the pond and dipped herself in it once. When she rose from the water, she was more beautiful than she could ever have imagined.

Excitedly, she dipped herself in the water again.

Now she was more richly dressed than any princess she had seen. She laughed aloud with joy as the bracelets and bangles on her arms jingled gaily. She examined the jewels and thought to herself, "One more time and I will be forever richer than Dukhu!"

One more time she dipped herself in the pond—though she had been warned not to do so.

When she rose from the water, she screamed madly as she watched all of the jewels melt away. Her nose grew long—as long as an elephant's trunk—and she was horribly ugly!

When Sukhu ran howling back to the old woman, the Mother of the Moon pointed to the three treasure chests. Sukhu grabbed the largest one and hobbled home.

Sukhu's mother almost fainted when she saw her daughter, but she hoped the large chest would hold some treasure.

Sukhu and her mother opened the box and out came an enormous black snake. It grew larger and larger and seemed to fill the room as it reared up, hissing loudly, ready to strike. They ran for their lives, and nobody ever saw them again.

Dukhu, on the other hand, lived happily with her husband and mother, wanting for nothing till the end of her days.

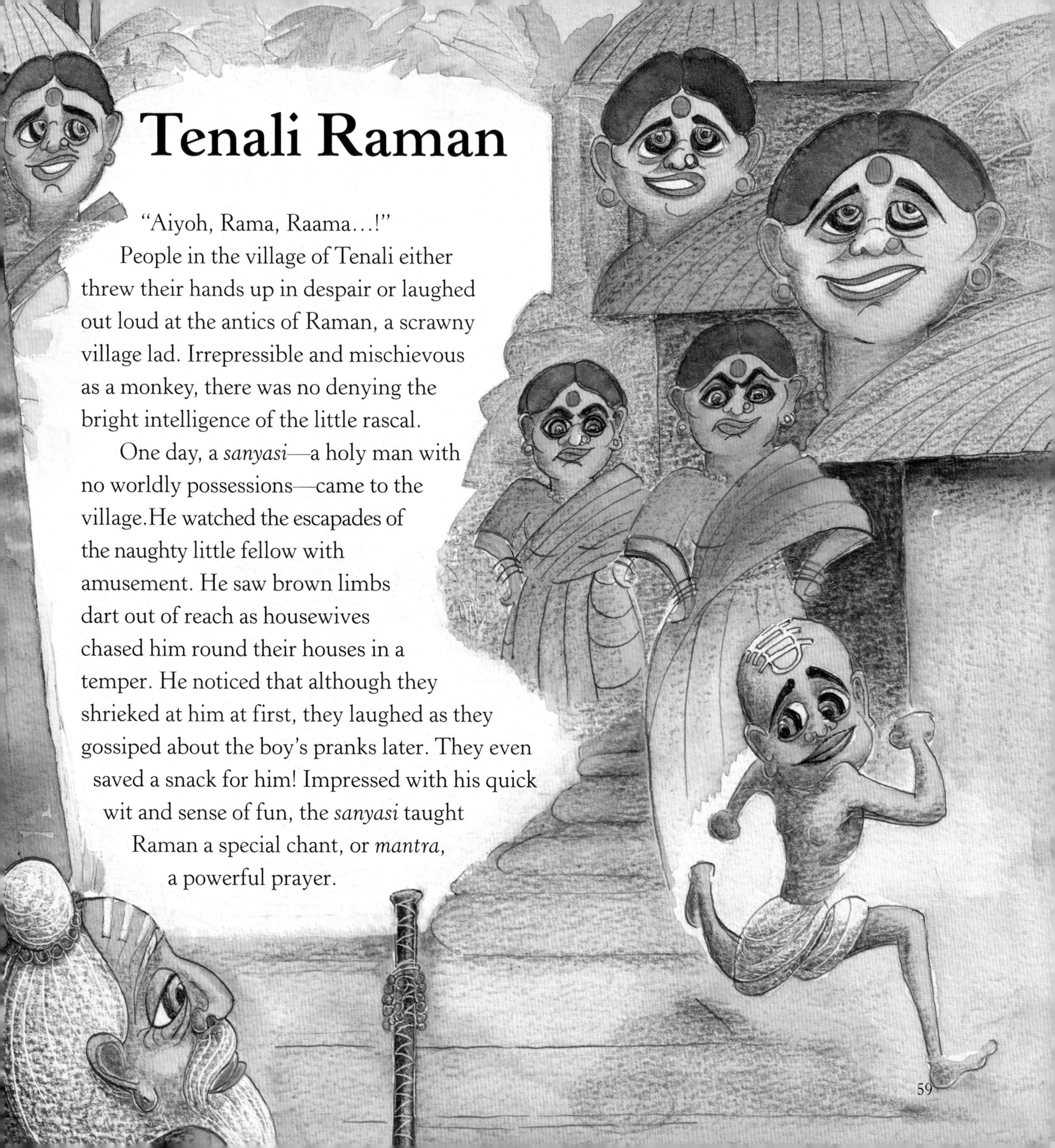

Tenali Raman

"Aiyoh, Rama, Raama...!"

People in the village of Tenali either threw their hands up in despair or laughed out loud at the antics of Raman, a scrawny village lad. Irrepressible and mischievous as a monkey, there was no denying the bright intelligence of the little rascal.

One day, a *sanyasi*—a holy man with no worldly possessions—came to the village. He watched the escapades of the naughty little fellow with amusement. He saw brown limbs dart out of reach as housewives chased him round their houses in a temper. He noticed that although they shrieked at him at first, they laughed as they gossiped about the boy's pranks later. They even saved a snack for him! Impressed with his quick wit and sense of fun, the *sanyasi* taught Raman a special chant, or *mantra*, a powerful prayer.

"Go alone at night to the temple of the fearsome goddess Kali. Repeat this *mantra* three million times and she will appear before you. Remember! The goddess has a thousand faces—each one is more frightful than the last. Grown men would tremble in terror at the sight of her, but you must not be afraid. If you can face her bravely, she will give you what you ask for."

Raman was determined to face Kali. He waited for the auspicious night.

The Kali temple was some distance away from the village. The path leading there wound round open fields and past a rocky outcrop before it went through the woods. The trees stood stiffly in the dark, their branches forming strange twisted shapes in the faint moonlight. All was still and silent as Raman stepped lightly over the uneven ground. A sudden gust of wind rustled the dry leaves in a whisper. An owl hooted nearby, and then a jackal howled in the distance. He hurried on and came out on the other side of the forest.

The temple was close to the cremation grounds. It loomed out of the darkness. Raman stared up at it, wondering if he was doing the right thing. *Be brave,* he told himself as he slipped in through the entrance.

Inside the temple, it was dark and shadowy. Pale moonlight filtered through the dusty skylight. Raman shut his eyes for a moment. Then slowly he opened them again and looked around.

Shrines to other gods and goddesses formed little niches with darker hollows. But, up ahead, he could make out the imposing black figure of the goddess Kali herself.

Keeping his eyes fixed on the idol, he walked right up to it. He examined it carefully. It was every bit as terrifying as people said it would be. But while many feared Kali, he knew that many others worshipped her.

Raman shut his eyes and began his holy chant. He had no idea how long it would take. He focused with all his might on doing it right. He repeated it, as he had been instructed, three million times.

Then he opened his eyes.

Slowly the figure in front of him began to gleam. The cold stone seemed to soften and breathe. Finally he was face to face with the goddess!

The idol came to life. It began to move and the one thousand faces of Kali began to flash before him in quick succession, each one more terrible than the other. The boy watched with fascination as the horrific figure grew larger and larger and larger.

But, by the time the one-thousandth face appeared, Raman was rolling on the floor and clutching his sides laughing!

The goddess was outraged. "You shameless little scallywag! How dare you laugh at me!"

Raman was unrepentant. Still giggling, he explained. "Oh Mother Kali, I honour you as I should. But it struck me that you have just two hands. When we humans get a cold, we have enough problems trying to keep our noses dry. Imagine if you should get a cold! However will you manage with just two hands and a thousand runny noses?"

The goddess was furious. "I shall punish you! For daring to laugh at me, you will have to earn a living for the rest of your life by making people laugh. You will be a jester, a clown, a *vikatakavi*!"

Raman paused for a minute to take a breath and consider what she had said. Then, he began to prance around the room chanting, "*Vi-ka-ta-ka-vi*! *Vi-ka-ta-ka-vi*! Oh! That is great! The sounds of the word form a palindrome. It sounds exactly the same, whether you say it from left to right, or the other way, from right to left!" And he continued to prance and chant mischievously.

No one could stay angry with Raman for long, not even the goddess Kali. After all, she had a sense of humour, too! She smiled and relented.

"A curse is a curse and it cannot be easily changed. You shall be a jester, a *vikatakavi*, just as I said. However, you will be no ordinary jester. You deserve to serve a king." Then the goddess disappeared.

That is how Tenali Raman, as the young boy came to be known, found his place at the court of the king of Vijayanagara. Perhaps it is because of the blessing of goddess Kali that people continue to enjoy his jokes to this very day!

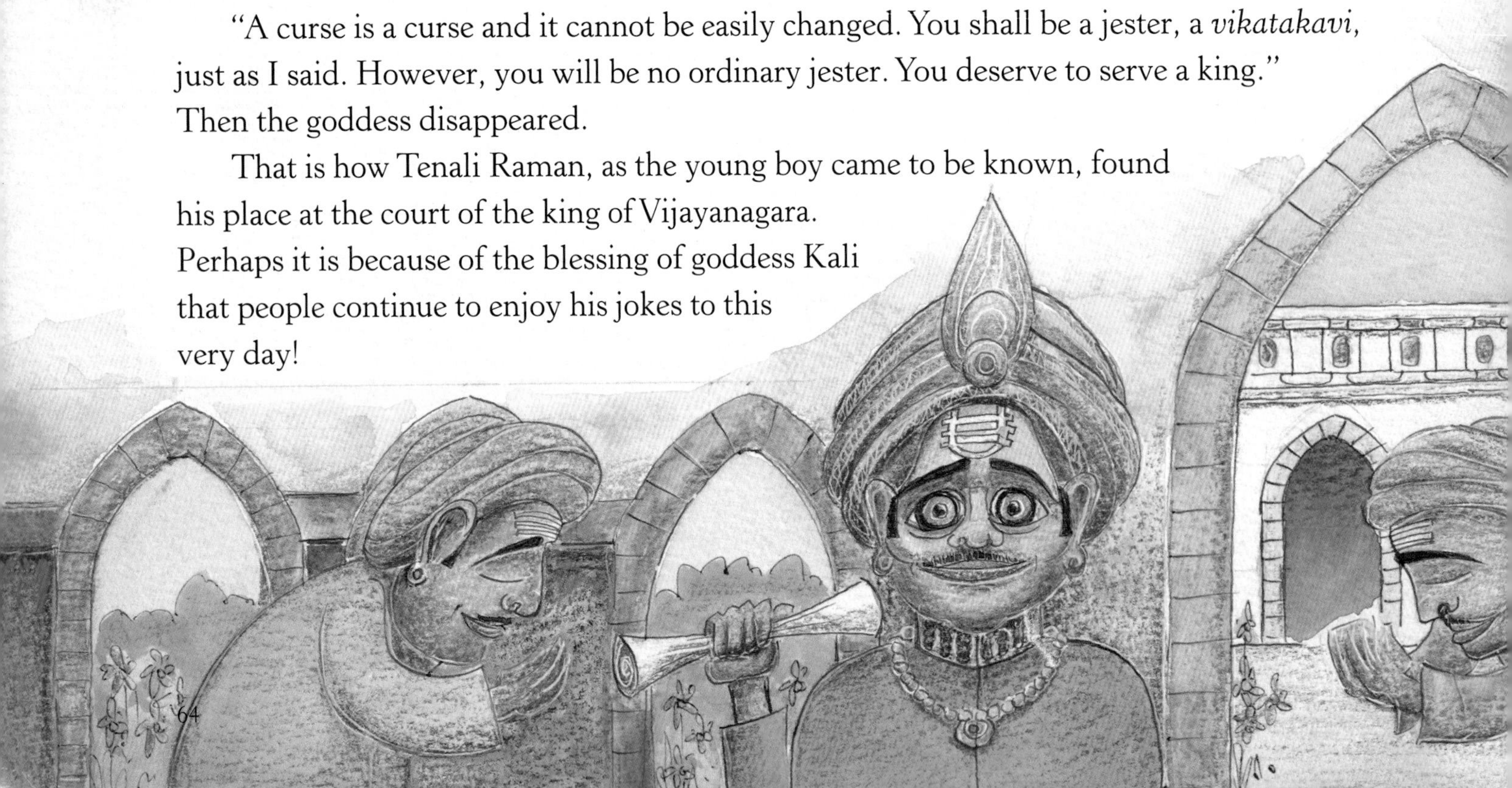

Journey to Heaven

Emperor Akbar's court was famous for its poets, musicians, philosophers and wise men of all sorts—and wisest of them all was Birbal. Birbal was Akbar's chief minister and closest friend.

But some in the court were jealous of the special place that Birbal held in the emperor's heart. They secretly plotted against Akbar and tried their best to get rid of Birbal.

These courtiers knew even if Akbar did not see through their plans, certainly Birbal was shrewd enough to do so. For this reason, they looked around for a stooge—someone foolish who could be tricked into doing the dirty work for them. Someone who would take the blame should anything go wrong. They found the royal barber—a vain, lazy and rather greedy man who lacked judgment and discretion.

They set to work on him.

They pretended to bump into the barber accidentally in the courtyard, and as they passed him, one of them would say,

"Salutations *Sahib*! Greetings! How are you today? Oh, you are a lucky man indeed. I have been trying to meet with the emperor for over a month and haven't succeeded yet. But you, you are guaranteed an audience with the emperor every day! You...and Birbal."

The barber was surprised and pleased. He realized it was true. He did get to see the emperor every day to groom his hair.

And on another day they would greet him saying, "*Salaams Sahib*! How goes it with you today? Ha! You smile, but what secrets do you carry in that well-groomed head of yours? You are fortunate indeed! You have a special place in the emperor's heart. You...and Birbal."

And they poked him in the back, friendly-like, and joked, "You are special indeed. The emperor must trust you. He allows you to come so close to him, and with a razor in your hand too! Ho, ho! You better watch out, people will become jealous of your power!"

The barber tried to laugh it off.

But then, they whispered in his ear. "Jokes aside, do you know that they say Birbal is jealous of you? You better be careful!"

And again, "I don't know how you look so calm. I wouldn't be able to sleep, or even close my eyes, if I knew that Birbal was jealous of me."

And finally they warned, "I hear Birbal is plotting against you. Watch out! Birbal is a dangerous man. A very dangerous man indeed!"

When they had frightened him enough, they persuaded him to try and get rid of Birbal. They whispered in his ear, "With Birbal out of the way, your future will be secure. In fact, you might never have to do another day of work. You could live like a prince yourself! Ha! Ha!"

Finally, the barber decided to do something.

The next morning, while shaving Emperor Akbar, the barber said, "Your Majesty, do you ever wonder how your father is doing in heaven?"

Akbar, who was a very practical man, answered, "What would be the point of that? Neither you, nor I, nor anybody else can ever know what is happening in heaven."

"Well, Your Highness," suggested the barber, "perhaps, you could send someone to find out."

"Yes, I could," laughed the emperor. "But the man would have to be dead to do that, wouldn't he? So how could he come back to report to me what he sees?"

"Well, Your Majesty," said the barber, carefully, "I have heard that there is a holy man—a *sadhu*, who lives deep in the jungle and has learnt how to send people to heaven."

"And how does he do that?" asked the emperor.

"The *sadhu* recites special prayers, and when the man is placed on a burning pyre, he rises with the ashes to heaven," answered the barber.

Akbar was now getting impatient with the barber. "Yes, but do they come back?"

"Oh yes, Your Majesty!" declared the barber confidently. "All the *sadhu* does is say the prayers backwards and he is able to bring them back."

"Whom should I send?" wondered the emperor aloud, looking meaningfully at the barber.

"Someone worthy of the task!" said the barber quickly. "The wisest man in the land—except for Your Majesty, of course. Someone like...Birbal!"

The emperor now knew that this was another plot against him, but he was curious to see how Birbal would deal with the challenge, so he summoned him.

"Birbal, listen carefully now. You are to go on an important journey—a journey to heaven. The barber has suggested that you go and see how my father is doing."

Akbar explained about the *sadhu*'s special skill. Birbal was no fool. He agreed to go immediately, but asked for a little time to get ready. "It will be a great honour, Your Majesty. However, for a journey of such importance, there are preparations to be made, gifts to be bought, rites and rituals to be observed."

The emperor agreed to his request.

A few weeks later, Birbal told the emperor he was ready. The royal procession set off from the palace to a lonely spot in the jungle. The barber was there, disguised as a holy man. The barber instructed that Birbal be laid on the pyre, which had been piled high with incense and fragrant sandalwood.

Then the barber, chanting loud prayers he had made up for the occasion, lit the fire. As the flames began to crackle and rise, the barber's accomplices began to chant loudly with him.

In the confusion of the prayers, chanting and smoke, clever Birbal escaped into a tunnel he had dug under the pyre. The tunnel led all the way through the jungle, back to his house.

Safe at home, Birbal was careful to stay indoors and let no one see him.

One day passed. Two days. A week. A month, and still Birbal had not returned.

The emperor was worried. Birbal had been his best friend!

Then, suddenly, Birbal appeared in the court. His long hair and beard looked untidy, but otherwise he seemed in good health and spirits.

The emperor was delighted. "Birbal, you are back! How is my father? What news do you bring?"

"Your father is well, Your Majesty," said Birbal, bowing low, "and delighted by the concern you show for his welfare."

"Is he happy? Does he need anything?" enquired the emperor.

"Your father is quite comfortable, Your Majesty. He lacks nothing except..."

"Except what?" demanded the emperor.

"Well, Your Majesty," replied Birbal, "as you can see from my long hair and beard, there isn't a single good barber in heaven. Your father wonders—if it is not too much trouble—whether you could send him one."

"My father should lack nothing!" declared the emperor promptly.

The barber was quickly summoned, put on a similar pyre and sent on his journey to heaven.

And that was the end of the barber.

The Foolish Man

Guruswami and his wife lived in the village. Oh, they were foolish! And, oh, were they stubborn! So foolish and stubborn, in fact, that they would argue all night over which one of them was the bigger fool.

A neighbour could not bear the noise they made any longer. He went up to them to try and settle the argument once and for all.

"Aiyoh, Swami! Neither of you is the biggest fool in the world. There are much bigger fools out there! If you don't believe me, go and see for yourselves."

Guruswami's wife, being perhaps the more stubborn of the two, did not believe their neighbour and so saw no reason to find out. But Guruswami thought all night about what the man had said.

The next morning, tying his turban firmly on his head, he set out to see the world. He wanted to find out for himself if what their neighbour had said was true.

He wandered around from village to village asking about the fools who lived there. Finally, someone told him about an entire village of idiots. When he went there, he found the villagers running around, carrying empty baskets in and out of their houses.

"What are you doing?" he asked.

"Oh," explained one villager, wearily mopping his brow, "it is a nice hot day, and the sun is shining bright. But our houses are dark, even at midday. So, we are trying to gather the sunlight in baskets to light up our homes. But it does not seem to be working very well."

Guruswami looked at their houses and thought quickly.

"Oh, that's easy," he said. "If you pay me, I will fill your houses with light."

The tired villagers quickly agreed. They paid him a hundred rupees.

Guruswami went into their houses and opened all the doors and windows.

Light soon poured into the houses. The villagers bowed down and touched his feet in respect.

As he walked on, Guruswami came to another curious sight. Several men—all of whom were tall, hefty and bulging with muscles—were trying to get the trunk of a tree into a house through a doorway that was far too small for it. They pushed and shoved, twisted and turned, but the trunk just would not go through. Finally they picked it up and ran into the doorway so hard that the entire house was in danger of falling down.

Guruswami offered to help—if they were willing to pay him. They agreed. Guruswami found that the tree trunk was to be used to make a wooden altar and furniture for the house. He arranged for the trunk to be sawed into smaller pieces, which were then carried into the house easily.

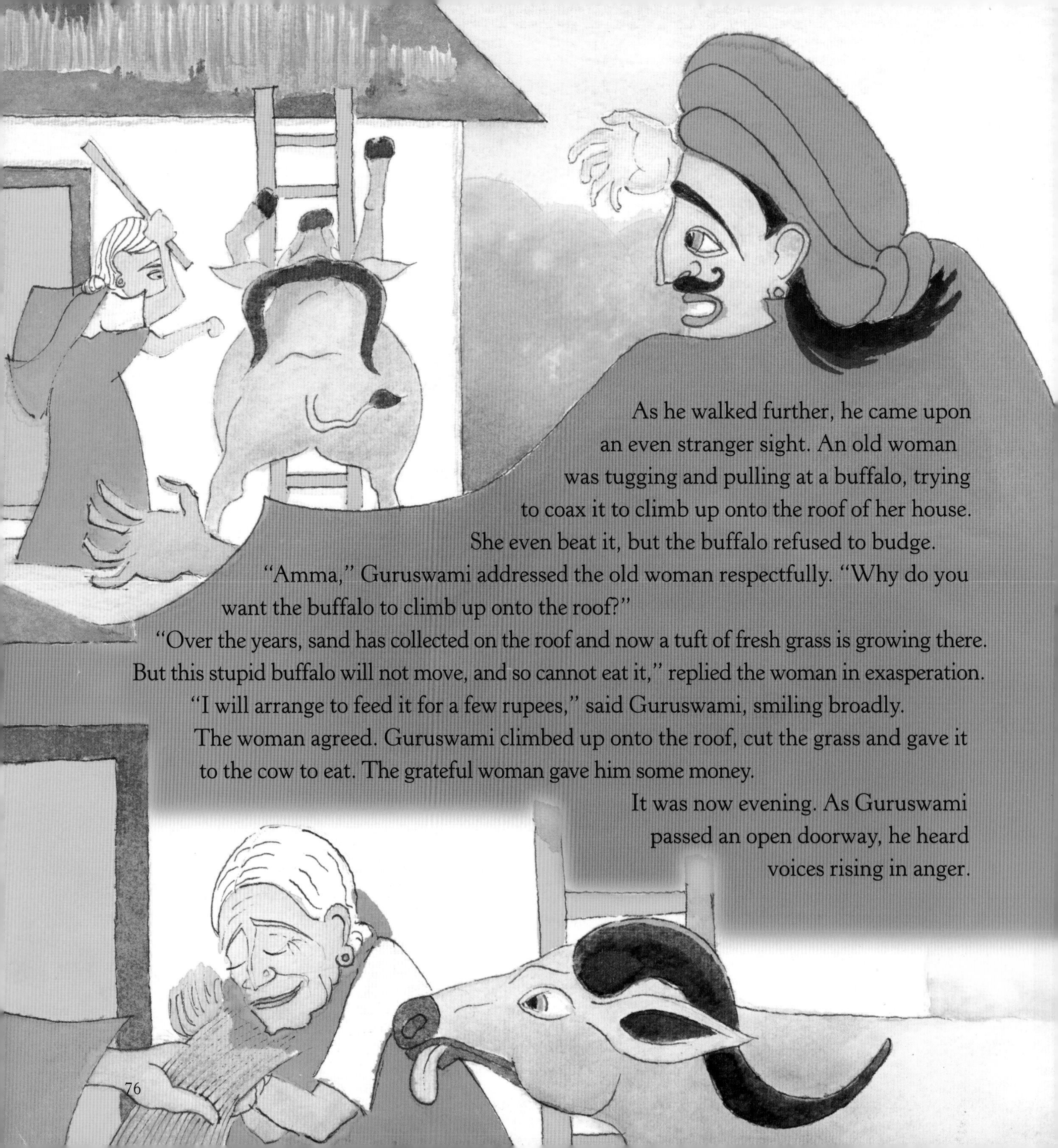

As he walked further, he came upon an even stranger sight. An old woman was tugging and pulling at a buffalo, trying to coax it to climb up onto the roof of her house. She even beat it, but the buffalo refused to budge.

"Amma," Guruswami addressed the old woman respectfully. "Why do you want the buffalo to climb up onto the roof?"

"Over the years, sand has collected on the roof and now a tuft of fresh grass is growing there. But this stupid buffalo will not move, and so cannot eat it," replied the woman in exasperation.

"I will arrange to feed it for a few rupees," said Guruswami, smiling broadly.

The woman agreed. Guruswami climbed up onto the roof, cut the grass and gave it to the cow to eat. The grateful woman gave him some money.

It was now evening. As Guruswami passed an open doorway, he heard voices rising in anger.

A husband and his wife were arguing about whose turn it was to shut the door.

"It's your turn!" shouted the husband.

"No, it isn't!" responded the wife furiously. "You opened it, so you shut it!"

This went on till both husband and wife were quite hoarse. Finally the husband said, "Well, neither of us can sleep unless we end this argument. So, let's settle on another way.

The first one who moves or speaks will have to shut the door. Do you agree?"

"Yes!" said the wife firmly. And then there was complete silence.

Guruswami waited for a while before tiptoeing through the doorway and entering the house. He found the couple in bed with their arms crossed, glaring at each other.

Through the corner of their eyes, they saw him but they did not speak a word. Instead they continued to challenge each other with their stares.

Guruswami walked around the room, examining everything in it. Neither husband nor wife said a word or moved.

Guruswami found a beautifully carved box in a drawer. It looked valuable. He opened it, and found that it was full of money—their life savings.

"Fate must have led me here for a reason," said Guruswami to the couple. "If neither of you has any objection, perhaps I should take this home with me? What do you say?"

Still, the husband and wife neither moved nor spoke.

Guruswami picked up the box and carried it out. The quarrelsome couple, not wanting to lose the argument, let him walk out of their home without saying a word!

But a moment later, he heard them shouting at each other, "You spoke first, so you shut the door!"

By this time, Guruswami had realized that he was certainly much smarter than he had thought. And that, he realized too, was a good thing.

He went home quite pleased with his newfound wealth and wisdom, stopped arguing with his wife, and lived happily for the rest of his life.

Glossary

Aiyoh, Rama, Ramaaa!: an exclamation for frustration which calls to God for help.

asura: the demons or titans who war against the devas in Hindu mythology. In the Vedic age, the asuras and devas were both considered classes of gods, but gradually they came to oppose each other.

auspicious: a time that is forecast to be favorable, often based on astrology.

cremation ground: the grounds where dead bodies are burnt to ashes.

gandharas: mythical beings, such as nature spirits who may be heavenly singers and musicians.

ghee: clarified butter, often used in traditional Indian sweets.

Kali: the female counterpart to Siva, God of Destruction. Often fearsome, she is a very complex deity and embodies many contrasts.

pyre: a large pile of wood on which a dead body is placed and burnt in funeral rites.

rakshasa: male demons who are among the most feared of all creatures in Hindu mythology. They are powerful creatures that can change to the forms of animals or humans. Rakshasas are fond of torturing human beings and have even been known to feast on them.

Salaams Sahib!: a respectful salutation, accompanied by a bow and a gesture of the hands.

swami: The word swami has many meanings including god. However, it is often used to refer to a teacher, especially a spiritual teacher such as a guru. In this story it is also a casual diminutive or short-form of the full name, Guruswami—which can be ironical, considering his foolishness.

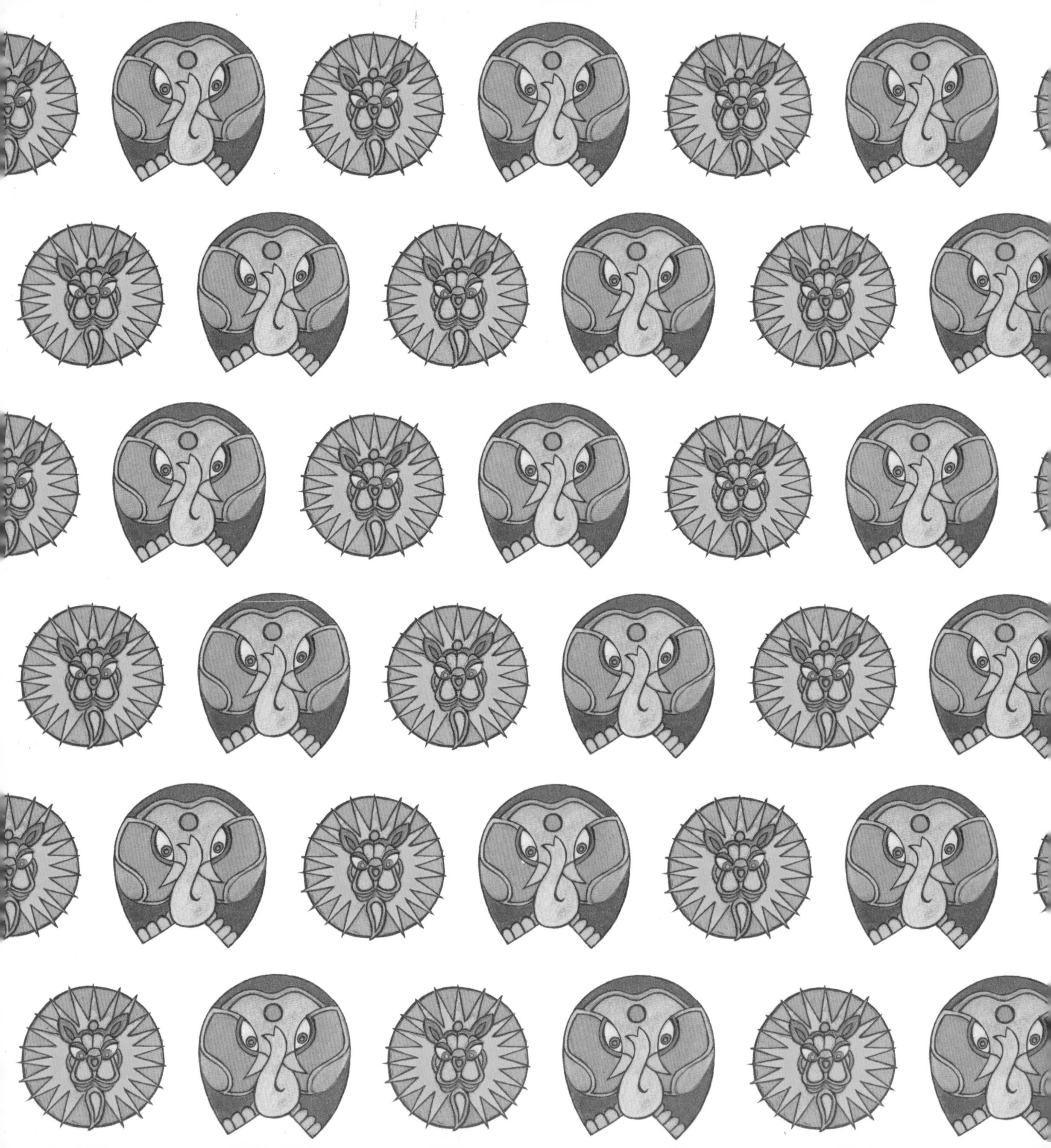